The Run,
Jump,
Bump
Book

The Run, Jump, Bump Book

by Robert Brooks

Illustrated by David M. McPhail

Little, Brown and Company

BOSTON   TORONTO

Published simultaneously in Canada
by Little, Brown & Company (Canada) Limited

PRINTED IN THE UNITED STATES OF AMERICA

For Kate

Not very long ago, in a tall brick building on a steep street near the middle of the city, lived a girl named Theresa.

Theresa was a city girl. When she went out for a drive in the country with her father and mother, she saw fields and farms and forests and the kinds of houses that other people lived in, but the part of the drive that Theresa really liked best was coming back to the city.

Because the city was special. The city was her home.

But some things about living in the city were hard.

One hard thing was how tall her building was.

It was not so tall that it needed an elevator, like some buildings. But it was four stories tall, and Theresa lived at the very top of it, in an apartment.

Since her building was four stories tall, it had three long flights of stairs.

Since Theresa lived at the top, she had to climb up all of them.

That was hard sometimes.

Other things were hard, too.

When she was inside her apartment at the top of all those stairs she could not say, "I think I will just step outside."

She could not just step outside.

Besides that, she was not even allowed to go out without her mother. So if her mother was too busy to go down all the stairs and outdoors, there was only one thing left to do. Play indoors.

That was what Theresa often did.

Now, indoors in Theresa's apartment there was not much extra space.

There was one short crooked hallway; her room went off it this way, and the

living room went off it that way. Her parents' room was next to the living room. The bathroom was across the hall. The kitchen was at the end.

And that was all.

In Theresa's room, everything was very close together.

That could be good. For instance, when she sat on her bed, she could reach every toy in her room without touching the floor.

Not so good was that as soon as she took something out, there was hardly enough room to play with it.

When Theresa set up her dinosaur farm, for instance, her room soon became very crowded.

The floor and the bed and the little night table in Theresa's room filled up quickly. By the time she had taken out the things that she needed, there was no place left for her to move without knocking them over.

So they got knocked over.

Then her mother would say, "Theresa, you had better do some picking up in there."

Theresa picked up her floor. She cleared off her bed and her table and put her toys and dolls and books in their places. Everything had its place.

Sometimes after she picked up her room she just had to clear the pigeons off the windowsill, too.

17

Then her mother would say, "Theresa. That's an outdoor noise."

So Theresa would ask, "Can we go outdoors now?"

"Not now. In a while."

In a while. What could she do till then?

In the living room she could skate a little on a magazine—as long as she missed the coffee table, and the lamps, and especially the geranium.

In her parent's room she could tumble
a little on the big bed—as long as her
father was not at the desk paying bills.

20

In the kitchen she could *not* jump rope, even a little.

Could she run? She tried.
Look out, cat! Look out, everybody!

Theresa could not run far in that apartment in the city, with all those walls and doors and halls and chairs and tables and cats . . . and people to run into.
That was hard, too.

Finally it would be time to go out.
Hooray!
But first she and her mother had to go down all those stairs . . .

and then stay right on the sidewalk so they wouldn't get run over . . .

and never cross the street until the light was green for them . . .

and they always had to be VERY CAREFUL.

Theresa and her mother would walk to the grocery. Then they would walk back up the hill to the house.

And sometimes that was all that happened.

But sometimes, *sometimes* it was different.

Staying very carefully on the sidewalk Theresa and her father would cross seven streets when the lights were green.

They would hurry through a traffic circle with cars pointing in every direction waiting for them.

They would climb up a long flight of stairs to a bridge for people over a river of cars.

They would cross the bridge. They would climb down the stairs on the other side.

Then suddenly there would be no more cars or lights or sidewalks, only trees and grass and the place that Theresa knew very well, where she could . . .

RUN

and JUMP

and BUMP

and *swing*

and *slide*

28

and *ride* the thing that
went round and round
for as long as she
liked . . . till it was
almost dark and
time to go back.

All over town the lights came on in windows
and signs and streetlamps.

Theresa and her father walked slowly toward
home over the bridge. It looked as if all the stars
in the sky had come down . . .

to live in the city.